In memory of my mum, who loved owls – J.H.

For Codie & Kyle – G.P.

First published 2022 by Macmillan Children's Books
an imprint of Pan Macmillan
The Smithson, 6 Briset Street, London EC1M 5NR
EU representative: Macmillan Publishers Ireland Limited, 1st Floor,
The Liffey Trust Centre, 117-126 Sheriff Street Upper, Dublin 1, D01 YC43
Associated companies throughout the world
www.panmacmillan.com

ISBN 978-1-5290-7050-7

Text copyright © John Hay 2022
Illustrations copyright © Garry Parsons 2022
Photographs © istock.com

1 3 5 7 9 8 6 4 2

A CIP catalogue record for this book
is available from the British Library.

Printed in China

John Hay

Garry Parsons

The Owl Who Came for Christmas

Macmillan Children's Books

It was night-time in the forest. Rosie the Screech Owl was out hunting. She spotted something wriggling on the forest floor. It was a delicious earthworm.

She swooped down, and picked it up.
"I'll save this one for dinner," she said,
and she hid it in a hole in the trunk of a fir tree.

As the sun came up, she snuggled
deep in the branches and fell asleep.

When Rosie woke, she knew something was wrong.
There was a roaring sound, the tree was swaying,
and then it fell to the ground. Rosie was frightened.

She squeezed her little body tight against the tree trunk
and shut her eyes so she looked just like part of the tree.

Someone dragged the tree through a netting machine, pulling the branches tight against the trunk.

Rosie was trapped.

Rosie heard chopping sounds and soon there were
lots of trees being loaded into the back of a lorry.

The engine rattled and the lorry rumbled away
from the forest and down a long road.

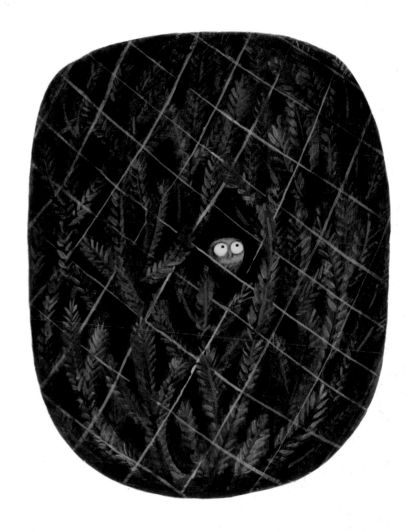

But poor Rosie was still nestled inside the tree, riding away on the lorry . . .

The next morning, Rosie heard voices near her tree.
"How about this one, Lily? It's really fresh!"
"And it smells like the forest, Mum!"
"Can we decorate it today?"

The family carried the tree to their car and tied it to the roof. Rosie felt the car moving and heard the sounds of the city. "Where am I?" wondered Rosie. "This is not the forest."

Mum, Lily and Ethan carried the tree into their house.
They opened their box of Christmas decorations and Lily
took out her favourites – baubles shaped like owls!
"I love owls," said Lily. "I'm going to put them everywhere!"

Lily peeped into the branches of the Christmas tree.
A little face stared back at her.

"That's funny," said Lily. "I thought I saw . . ."
Rosie shut her eyes, squeezed back against the trunk
and pretended she was part of the tree.

After decorating the tree, Mum, Dad, Lily and Ethan sat down for their dinner.

But Rosie the owl had no dinner.

It was days since she had eaten the worm she had caught in the forest. She squeezed through the branches and peered out into the room, looking for snacks.

"I'm just going to look at the Christmas tree again," said Lily after dinner.

She skipped through the house and then stopped in her tracks.

Lily looked at Rosie.
Rosie stared back.

"Mum, look!" called Lily.
"There's a bauble moving
in the tree!"

Mum went to look. Rosie heard her footsteps, and turned her head. Mum jumped. "That's not a bauble," she said. "That's a real . . . live . . . tiny . . . OWL!"

"What are we going to do?" asked Ethan.
"Should we help her to get out?" asked Lily.
"No," said Dad, "let's try not to frighten her."

They opened the garden doors near the tree, turned off the lights and went to bed. Perhaps the little owl would just fly away into the night . . .

But later, when Dad tiptoed into the room, he found Rosie perched at the very top of the tree, fast asleep.

Next morning, Mum called the local wildlife centre.
"You'll never believe this," she said, "but we've got a little
owl living in our Christmas tree!"

"An owl in a Christmas tree? I need to see this," said the
wildlife expert.

She brought some food for the owl and set it down amongst the branches.
"Ooh, good," thought Rosie.
"I was really peckish."

After her meal Rosie felt sleepy. She didn't mind when the wildlife lady picked her up and gently put her in a box.

When Rosie woke up, she was outside.
It was dark and it was hunting time.

She hopped on to the edge of the box and looked around.

There was a plate with some more food on the ground.
"I'll just have a quick snack before I go," she thought.

Later that evening, when Lily and Ethan went out into the garden, the owl had gone!

Next day, it was Christmas Eve. The children were hanging their stockings, the Christmas tree was covered with beautiful decorations, but there was something missing.

They went to the window.
"Look!" said Lily. "There she is!"

And there, in the moonlit sky, they saw a swish of wings
as the little owl made her way home.

"Happy Christmas, Little Owl," said Lily.

One Christmas, a family in America really did find an owl nestled in their Christmas tree. It was a tiny owl, about the size of a robin, with red-brown feathers and tufted ears, known as an Eastern Screech Owl.

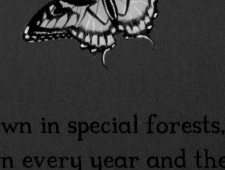

Christmas trees are grown in special forests, where trees are cut down every year and then replanted. The poor little owl must have been roosting in one of the trees when it was cut down - ending up a long way from home!

If they feel frightened, Eastern Screech Owls like Rosie are very good at hiding in trees. They tuck their wings in tight and stretch their bodies out, and the speckled pattern on their feathers helps camouflage them against the bark.

So no one noticed the owl until the tree was up and decorated, and a little face peeked out. At first, the family waited to see if their unexpected Christmas visitor would fly away . . . but she didn't move, so they called their local wildlife centre for help.

In the wild, owls hunt for tasty treats, such as snails, worms, mice and even frogs. The poor Christmas tree owl hadn't eaten for days, so they put some raw chicken out for her.

Then they took the little owl outside in a box and set her free – back to the forest, after her big adventure.